On the Luck of an Irish Sailor

For Wade,
May you be always
be lucky!

On the Luck of an Irish Sailor

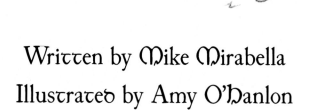

Written by Mike Mirabella

Illustrated by Amy O'Hanlon

LUCKYSAILORPRODUCTIONS

For informaion regarding permission,
write to Mike Mirabella at mike@papamikesmusic.com

Music:
Copyright © 1976 & 2013 Michael Mirabella
Music in the version pages 29–32 by Erik Hoffman, 2013

Author: Michael Mirabella
Edited by: Wendy Waits, Steve Kirby, Wendy Alioto,
         Charylu Roberts, Bob Cooper
Illustrator: Amy O'Hanlon
Cover design, interior design by Amy O'Hanlon
Book production: Jim Shubin

ISBN: 978-0-9972642-6-5

First Printing 2016
Printed in the United States of America

The song *On the Luck of a Irish Sailor* and the book are available at: LUCKYSAILORPRODUCTIONS
www.papamikesmusic.com

On the Luck of an Irish Sailor

story-song written by Mike Mirabella, recorded with the voice of the legendary Shay Black

I dedicate *On the Luck of an Irish Sailor* to

my proud part-Irish mother who believed

that green was the only color to wear,

that family attendance at Saint Patrick's Day dinners was

as mandatory as a holy day of obligation.

For my Mother
ELEANOR

A salty old jack back in my youth,
Would tell me stories of the ocean blue;
Had a melon of a belly and a hole in his shoe,
his coat needed mending and his socks did too.

Lie dee dee, lie dee doo,
Oh, for the life on the ocean blue;
I believe in a wish come true,
On the luck of an Irish Sailor.

Told of a time he was lost at sea,
Cast adrift in the briny deep;
A puff on his pipe and a cup o' cheer,
Spoke in a manner that was quite sincere.

"There's three days out o' Macoo Bay,
The sea grew dark and the sky turned grey;
The wind blew fierce to a mighty gale,

when WHACK went the SPLASH of
a mermaid's tail.

The waves rolled over and the ship went down,
Thar for certain that I be drowned;
When up popped the top of a mermaid's head,
The mermaid smiled and to me she said,

'Lie dee dee, lie dee doo,
Oh, for the life on the ocean blue;
I believe in a wish come true,
On the luck of an Irish Sailor.'

She called me name, she took me hand,
Down to the bottom of the sea we swam;
'Now sailor, there's no need to fear,
'Tis Irish Luck that's got you here.'

Hair be blue, her eyes be green,
The darlin' daughter of a mermaid queen;
We all sat 'round at a royal feast,
Where the sand dabs danced
to a rock cod beat.

The scallops, clams and giant snails,
Told lobster jokes and fishy tales;
We laughed and sang, I tell you true,

Stayed full year, lad, well,
wouldn't you?

Lie dee dee, lie dee doo,
Oh, for the life on the ocean blue;
I believe in a wish come true,
On the Luck of an Irish Sailor.

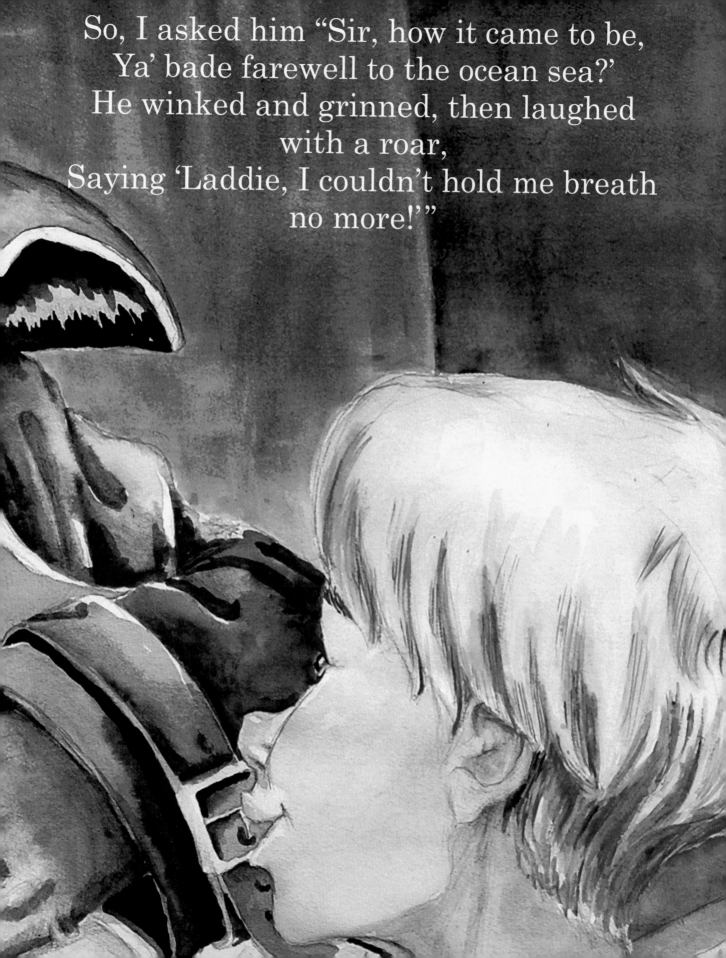

So, I asked him "Sir, how it came to be,
Ya' bade farewell to the ocean sea?'
He winked and grinned, then laughed
with a roar,
Saying 'Laddie, I couldn't hold me breath
no more!'"

Lie dee dee, lie dee doo,
Oh, for the life on the ocean blue,
I believe in a wish come true,
On the luck of an Irish Sailor.

Lie dee dee, lie dee doo,
Oh, for the life on the ocean blue;
I believe every word was true,
On the luck of an Irish Sailor.

On the Luck of an Irish Sailor

Words by
MIKE MIRABELLA

Original Music by **ERIK HOFFMAN**
and **MIKE MIRABELLA**

A salt-y old jack back in my youth, would tell me stor-ies of the o-cean blue; had a

mel-on of a bel-ly, and a hole in his shoe, coat need-ed mend-ing and his socks did too!_____

Chorus

Lie dee dee, lie dee doo, oh, for the life on the o-cean blue;

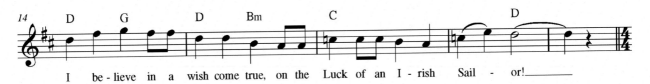

I be-lieve in a wish come true, on the Luck of an I-rish Sail - or!_____

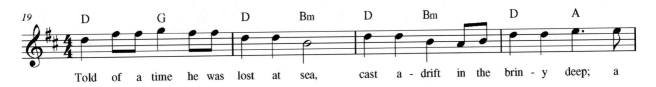

Told of a time he was lost at sea, cast a-drift in the brin-y deep; a

puff on his pipe, and a cup o' cheer, spoke in a man-ner that was quite sin - cere._____

_____ 'There's three days out o'

Ma-coo Bay, the sea grew dark and the sky turned grey; the wind blew fierce to a

© 1976 - 2012 by Bay Mike's Music (ASCAP)

rock cod beat._____ The scal- lops, clams, and gi - ant snails told

lob - ster jokes and fish - y tails; we laughed and sang, I

Chorus

tell you true, stayed full year, lad, well, would-n't you?___ Lie dee dee,

lie dee doo, oh, for the life on the o - cean blue; I be - lieve in a

wish come true, on the Luck of an I - rish Sail - or!___

Traditional Tune

On the Luck of an Irish Sailor

So I asked him, 'Sir, how it came to be, ya bade fare-well to the o-cean sea?' He winked and grinned, then laughed with a roar, say-ing, 'Lad-die,____ I could-n't hold me breath no more!'

Chorus

Lie dee dee, lie dee doo, oh, for the life on the o-cean blue; I be-lieve in a wish come true, on the Luck of an I-rish Sail - or!_____

Lie dee dee, lie dee doo, oh, for the life on the o-cean blue; I be-lieve ev-'ry word was true, on the Luck of an I-rish Sail - or!

Traditional Tune

About the Music

On The Luck Of An Irish Sailor is a story-song written by Mike Mirabella, recorded with the voice of legendary Shay Black, the eldest of Ireland's renown Black Family. Shay IS the voice that Mike heard in his mind when writing the text more than 50 years ago. The melody of 'Sailor' is an infusion of Mike's vision, the creative efforts of master musician and teacher Erik Hoffman, and recognizable riffs of traditional Irish Folk music. *On The Luck Of An Irish Sailor* was recorded with authentic Irish folk instruments and was co-produced with Mike by twice Grammy Award certificated winner Jim Nunally, at Nunally's recording studio in Crockett CA.

Erik Hoffman resides in Oakland California and is a master musician on an assortment of folk string instruments. He is also a much sought-after contra and square dance teacher and caller. Erik also teaches fiddle at the Freight and Salvage Coffeehouse in Berkeley CA. and is a regular dance caller at the annual California Bluegrass Association Music Camps as well as other Northern California venues.

Because of his versatile musicianship and vast knowledge of Celtic music, Erik was asked to collaborate on 'On The Luck Of An Irish Sailor' as its primary composer and music coordinator.

Shay Black is an avid songcatcher, musician and singer and is known for his extensive knowledge of songs and music from the Irish, English and Scottish traditions. Born in Dublin, Ireland, he moved in 1994 to Berkeley, CA from Liverpool.

Shay is the eldest member of Ireland's Black Family, who are "regarded as one of the most impressive groups of Irish singers to be found anywhere" according to a recent review in The Irish Echo. The Black Family includes his brothers Michael and Martin and sisters Frances and Mary Black.

Shay teaches Folk Repertoire at Berkeley's Freight and Salvage music venue and his most regular local gig is the weekly Starry Irish Music Session at the Starry Plough pub in Berkeley.

About the Author

"Papa" Mike Mirabella is a retired public school teacher who resides with his wife in the San Francisco Bay Area. He is an accomplished guitar player who thinks of himself as primarily a singer-songwriter. Mike wrote the text of *On The Luck Of An Irish Sailor* when he was 15 years old, but it wasn't until 50 years later that Mike was encouraged to develop 'Irish Sailor' into a children's book and sound recording.

"Papa" Mike is a long time writer-composer known for his children's songs, "Sister Butterfly", "I Am So Like You" and "I Used To Be Shy". He also penned such popular Christian songs as "Special People" and "My Jesus Rose On Easter Morning".

About the Illustrator

Amy O'Hanlon is an illustrator from the San Francisco Bay Area. She began studying art at Humboldt State University of California before continuing her education at Kingston University in London where she graduated with distinction in 2015. *On the Luck of an Irish Sailor* was her first children's book. Amy has since gone on to several other projects including her own book called "The Robot Kid," a story about feeling loss.

Amy is inspired by the fantasy of everyday life, that magic that exists just in the corner of your eye. She is drawn to stories that look beneath the surface, that have surprising depth and emotional intelligence. Those are the stories that drive her to create art.

S

Made in the USA
San Bernardino, CA
13 February 2017

Children's Fiction $16.95

On the Luck of an Irish Sailor

By Mike Mirabella

On The Luck of an Irish Sailor is a fantasy tale of how a young Irish sailor, while cast adrift in the ocean sea, is then saved from drowning by both the efforts of a mermaid princess and his Irish luck.

The tale was inspired by the stories I heard as a little boy while sitting at the kitchen table at our large Italian family dinners. My grandpa and uncles would tell tales of fishing the waters off the Coast of California and up through the inland passages of Alaska. I recall my grandpa Angelo telling of the scary time when he was a cabin boy of 12, and was captured by pirates while working on the tall ships. And then there was the neverending argument of whether the strange creature my grandpa and my uncle Cam had caught off the coast of Alaska was either a mermaid or a merman.

I was (and still am), that wee lad in our story, sitting wide-eyed and half-believing, but never tiring of hearing those wonder filled stories told by those 'salty old jacks'.

"Papa" Mike Mirabella is a retired public school teacher who resides with his wife in the San Francisco Bay Area. He is an accomplished guitar player who thinks of himself as primarily a singer-songwriter. Mike wrote the text of *On The Luck of an Irish Sailor* when he was 15 years old, but it wasn't until 50 years later that Mike was encouraged to develop 'Irish Sailor' into a children's book and recording.

ISBN: 978-0-9972642-6-5

51695

9 780997 264265